Developed by Nancy Hall, Inc. Designed by Eleanor Kwei.
Typeset in Mrs. Eaves and Belwe Mono LET.
Book printed and assembled in Malaysia for Hall Associates, Inc., New York, N.Y.
Charms and bracelet made in the United States of America. Conforms to ASTM F963-95
and EN71 requirements. ISBN: 0-8118-2361-X

Distributed in Canada by Raincoast Books
860 Cambie Street, Vancouver, British Columbia V6P 6M9

10 9 8 7 6 5 4 3 2 1

Chronicle Books
85 Second Street
San Francisco, California 94105

www.chroniclebooks.com

Princess Daisy
FINDS A FRIEND

by Kirsten Hall ❀ Illustrated by G. Brian Karas

chronicle books · san francisco

Once upon a time, there lived a princess named Daisy who had everything a little girl could possibly want. Her tower was filled with toys. She had more dresses than the queen herself. Yet Daisy never smiled.

The king and queen wondered what could be wrong. Did Daisy need a pet dragon or a diamond tiara? Would she smile if she had her very own circus? Her parents tried everything they could think of to cheer her up, but nothing seemed to work!

At night, while everyone
slept, Princess Daisy climbed
out of her bed and sat by her
window. She wished upon
a star for the one thing
she did not have—
a friend of her own.

Daisy didn't want to play with boys and girls who curtseyed every time they saw her. She didn't want someone who let her win at every game she played. Daisy wanted a real friend.

One morning, the princess awoke to the sound of a beautiful song.
She slipped on her velvet robe and hurried to the window where she
spotted a peasant girl singing and picking flowers in the royal garden.

Princess Daisy ran to her closet and pushed aside her silken slips and velvet gowns. Finally she put on her simplest dress. She pulled the collar off and tore loose the hem. Standing before the mirror, Daisy hardly recognized herself.

Then she tiptoed downstairs. Just as she approached the garden door, a servant entered. Daisy's heart began to pound, but the servant paid no attention to her.

Daisy ran through the open door into the garden. "Hello," she said shyly to the little girl. "You have a beautiful voice. And I like your flower crown."

"Thank you," said the little girl. "My name is Annie, and I can make you a crown, too."

Daisy sat very still as Annie wove the flowers into her hair. Daisy was so excited. She had worn diamonds and rubies and silver barrettes in her hair, but never flowers!

When they were done, Daisy spun in a circle. She had never felt so happy. Annie began to giggle and spin, too. Soon the girls were running hand in hand across the meadow.

They were so happy to have found each other that the girls hardly even noticed a family of rabbits nibbling away in a nearby lettuce patch.

When the afternoon sun grew hot, the girls splashed each other in the palace pond.

As the sun began to set, the girls headed back toward the castle, playing all the way. But when they reached the palace lawn, they heard a terrible commotion.

Suddenly, the girls were surrounded by the royal servants.

"Your Highness! Are you all right?" they asked in alarm.

The king and queen rushed toward Daisy. Their relief at discovering her turned into amazement. Daisy was smiling.

Annie was stunned. "You . . . You are the princess? . . ."

"Yes, I am Princess Daisy. I didn't want you to know. I wanted you to like me for myself, so we could be real friends."

"We already are," Annie answered.

Daisy smiled. "Best friends."

To celebrate their friendship, Daisy gave Annie a golden charm bracelet. "I'll wear it always," said Annie.

And Princess Daisy was never sad again.